First published by Parragon in 2012
Parragon
Chartist House
15–17 Trim Street
Bath BA1 1HA, UK
www.parragon.com

Edited by: Gemma Louise Lowe
Designed by: Jim Willmott
Production by: Jack Aylward

ISBN 978-1-78186-037-3

Printed in China

MICKEY MOUSE CLUBHOUSE

PaRRagon

Bath · New York · Singapore · Hong Kong · Cologne · Delhi
Melbourne · Amsterdam · Johannesburg · Shenzhen

Donald and his friends were standing outside the
Clubhouse on a crisp, bright day.

"Oh, Donald," Daisy said, "look at the sky! It's lovely!"

"Shhh!" Donald whispered. "Don't make a move!
Something is following me, and I'm going to find out who –
or what – it is!"

Daisy giggled as she looked behind Donald.

"Oh, my!" said Daisy. "There is something following you! It's wearing a sailor's cap – just like yours. It's got cute webbed feet – just like yours. And when you move, it moves, too."

"Aw, phooey," Donald quacked as he turned around and saw his shadow. "That is a fine-looking shape, but I still don't trust it!"

The friends laughed at Donald as he glared at his shadow. "Cheer up, buddy," Mickey said. "Why don't you leave your shadow on the ground and come with me?"

"I don't know." Donald moped. "Where are we going?"

"Up, up and away!" Mickey cheered. "Who wants to help Minnie and me fly our hot-air balloon?"

"I sure do!" shouted Goofy.

"You can count me out," Donald grumbled. "I don't trust that thing. Besides," he added, "I'm not missing lunch."

"Aw, come on, Donald," Minnie pleaded, "I've packed a square meal for each of us. Up, up and away!"

"Something's wrong," Mickey said. "The balloon won't fill with air!"

"That's too bad, buddy," said Donald, trying to hide a grin. "I guess we'll just have to go back to the Clubhouse for lunch."

"Oh, Toodles!" Mickey said. "Do we have a Mousketool that can help?" Toodles appeared. "Do any of you know how we can use this tool?" Mickey asked.

"I know, Mickey!" answered Minnie. "We can turn the crank to inflate the balloon with hot air."

"Why, you're right, Minnie!" Mickey shouted. "We've got ears! Say cheers!"

Soon, the friends were floating high above the Clubhouse. "Up, up and away!" cried Daisy. "This is fun!"

"Look, everyone!" yelled Minnie. "Can you see the Clubhouse from here? It looks so small! And there are so many shapes below us. I see a heart, a triangle and a rectangle. What do you see?"

"I see a triangle, too!" Mickey shouted. "And there are Chip and Dale playing a round of golf!"

"It should be called a triangle of golf," laughed Daisy. "Just look at all those triangle-shaped flags!"

"What's a triangle?" asked Goofy, as he bit into his sandwich.

"A triangle is a shape with three sides that all have points at the ends – sort of like your sandwich," Minnie explained.

"Or like that?" Goofy questioned, as he pointed to a huge triangle in front of the balloon.

It was the top of a mountain! Suddenly, a gust of wind whisked the friends right towards it!

"We need help," cried Mickey. "Oh, Toodles!"

Toodles appeared with a triangle, a patch, a ladder, and a spyglass.

"Which tool should we use?" asked Minnie.

"Let's try them all!" said Mickey. "Daisy, ring the triangle for help!"

Daisy rang the triangle, but it didn't help them get off the mountain.

"Minnie, patch the hole!"

Minnie put a square patch on the round hole in the balloon, but it was too small.

"Goofy, look through the spyglass!" Goofy held the spyglass and saw that the ground looked very far away.

"There's only one tool left," yelled Mickey. "To the ladder!"

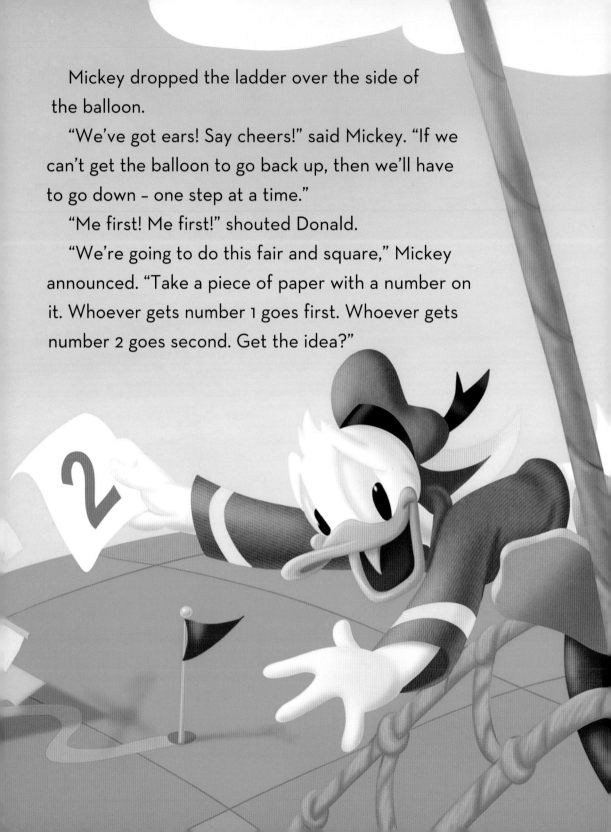

Mickey dropped the ladder over the side of the balloon.

"We've got ears! Say cheers!" said Mickey. "If we can't get the balloon to go back up, then we'll have to go down – one step at a time."

"Me first! Me first!" shouted Donald.

"We're going to do this fair and square," Mickey announced. "Take a piece of paper with a number on it. Whoever gets number 1 goes first. Whoever gets number 2 goes second. Get the idea?"

The friends headed down the ladder one by one.
Everyone was happy to be standing on firm ground again.
"We're in great shape, unlike our balloon," said Mickey.
"But we're going to have to hike back home. It's not far
- just down that path ... or maybe it's that other one...."

The friends trudged along, growing more and more tired.
"I think we've been walking in circles," Mickey finally said.
"I'm sure I've seen this tree before."

"Oh, Toodles!"

Toodles appeared, showing three pictures of Mickey. Mickey shared them with his friends. "I'm standing in front of the Clubhouse and my shadow is different in each picture. In the morning, my shadow falls in front of me. At noon, I have no shadow. In the evening, my shadow falls behind me. Do any of you know what this could mean?"

The friends studied the pictures carefully.

"I've got it!" Donald shouted. "Right now, it's late and the sun is setting behind us. Toodles shows that in the evening, our shadows point toward the Clubhouse. If we follow them, they'll lead us back home."

Donald was right. The shadows helped the friends head in the right direction. Soon, they arrived back at the Clubhouse. Everyone was hungry from the long trip.

"Well, Donald," Daisy said, "do you trust your shadow now?"

"I'll trust the handsome guy to lead me home," Donald answered. "But he better not ask me to share my pie!"